THE WORLD'S TOP TEN

CITIES

Neil Morris

ILLUSTRATED BY VANESSA CARD

RSVP

RAINTREE
STECK-VAUGHN
PUBLISHERS
The Steck-Vaughn Company

Austin, Texas

Words in **bold** are explained in the glossary
on pages 30–31.

Published by Raintree Steck-Vaughn Publishers, an imprint
of Steck-Vaughn Company.

Editors: Maria O'Neill, Heather Luff
Designer: Dawn Apperley
Picture researcher: Dianna Morris
Consultant: Elizabeth M. Lewis

Picture acknowledgments:
J Allan Cash: 4, 9, 21, 23. James Davis Photography: 5, 15,
20, 22. Eye Ubiquitous: 18. Robert Harding Picture Library:
11, 12, 13, 19, 26. Hutchison Picture Library: 14. Rex
Features: 17, 27. Tony Stone Images: 10, 28b, 28t, 29b.
Trip: 25, 28t. Zefa: 8, 16, 24.

Library of Congress Cataloging-in-Publication Data
Morris, Neil.
    Cities / Neil Morris; illustrated by Vanessa Card.
      p.   cm. — (The world's top ten)
    Includes index.
    Summary: A basic overview of the ten most populated
cities in the world, including Tokyo, New York, and
Mexico City.
    ISBN 0-8172-4344-5
    1. Cities and towns — Juvenile literature. [1. Cities
and towns.] I. Card, Vanessa, ill. II. Title. III. Series.
HT152.M67 1997
307.76 — dc20   96-30119
                                          CIP AC

Printed in China
Bound in the United States
1 2 3 4 5 6 7 8 9 0 LB 00 99 98 97 96

Contents

What Is a City?

A city is a very large town, where thousands of people live and work. The world's largest cities have millions of **inhabitants**. Some ancient cities, such as Rome and Athens, are still important national capitals today. Other newer cities, such as São Paulo and Bombay, are growing faster as more people move there from country areas or from other towns.

The Colosseum in Rome, the capital of Italy, was built almost 2,000 years ago. In those days the city already had about a million residents. Rome is called the Eternal City because it has survived for so long.

More people, more cities

The number of people in the world is growing by over 200,000 every day. In 1950 less than one-third of the world's population lived in towns. By 1995 the number had grown to almost half, and it will be nearly three-quarters by 2025.

There are now many huge cities, and most are getting bigger all the time. At the beginning of this century, 16 cities had over a million inhabitants. Now there are about 300 cities with a million people throughout the world.

4

Bigger and bigger

Cities grow outward from the center. Since **skyscrapers** were first built over a hundred years ago, many cities have also grown upward. At the center of a city there are large stores, offices, and banks. In this inner city area, when older buildings decay, new offices and businesses take their place.

In the outer city, there are often many businesses and small factories, as well as houses and apartment buildings. The **suburbs,** where many city-dwellers have their homes, are even farther out.

Jakarta, the capital of Indonesia, is one of the world's fastest growing cities. With more than eight million people, this modern city has grown three times bigger in the last thirty years.

The biggest cities

In this book we take a look at the ten cities in the world that have the largest populations. We find out how they began, learn how they grew, and see how they look today. We discover how different they are from each other, and we get to know the people who have made these cities their home.

This diagram shows the different parts of a typical city and how they are linked together.

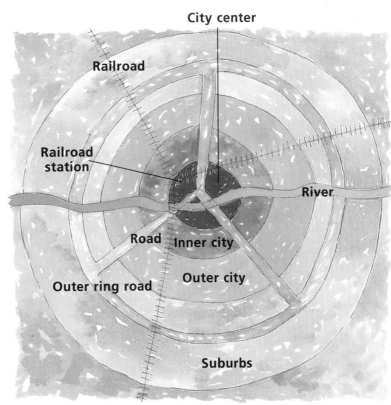

City center

Railroad

Railroad station

River

Road   Inner city

Outer city

Outer ring road

Suburbs

5

The Biggest Cities

The map shows where the ten biggest cities are in the world. Tokyo, New York, and Los Angeles are in wealthy countries north of the **Equator**. The other cities are all in less wealthy countries. Big cities are growing faster in these poorer regions of the world.

The population figure given for each city in this book means the number of people living in the "greater city." This includes the city's suburbs and the surrounding built-up areas. Sometimes other cities are included in the greater city.

A huge spread of cities that have grown until they join each other is called a **conurbation**.

The World's Top Ten Cities

1 Tokyo	25,000,000	people
2 São Paulo	18,100,000	people
3 New York	18,000,000	people
4 Mexico City	15,100,000	people
5 Los Angeles	14,500,000	people
6 Shanghai	13,400,000	people
7 Cairo	13,300,000	people
8 Bombay	12,600,000	people
9 Buenos Aires	12,500,000	people
10 Rio de Janeiro	11,100,000	people

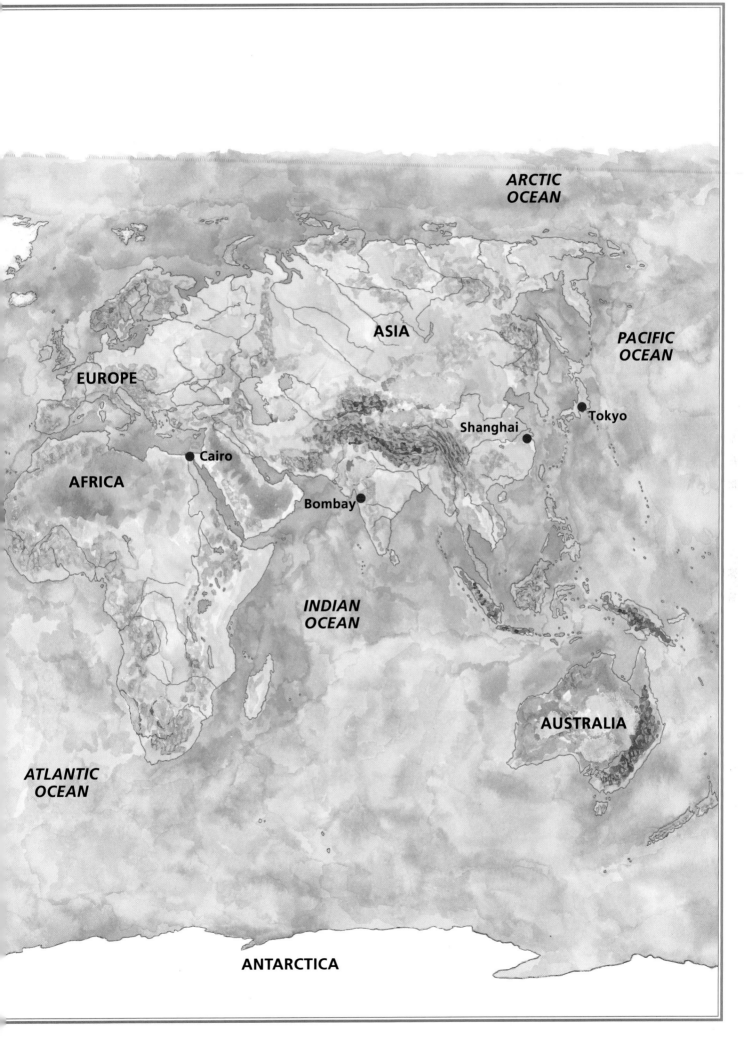

Tokyo

Tokyo is the capital of Japan. It lies next to Tokyo Bay on the eastern coast of Honshu, the largest of the Japanese islands. The conurbation covers an enormous region made up of different districts, towns, and cities that lie next to each other. This huge built-up area is home to 25 million people, making Tokyo the biggest city in the world.

A view over the crowded Shibuya district toward the Tokyo Tower, the city's tallest structure, which rises to 1,093 feet (333 m). Shibuya is full of stores and offices.

City of cities

In Tokyo individual cities have grown so big that they meet each other. There is now no countryside left between them. Central Tokyo has almost 12 million people. Nearby on Tokyo Bay is the industrial city of Kawasaki, where more than a million people live. Farther along the bay more than 3 million people live in Yokohama, where the capital's deepwater harbor is found.

Eastern capital

The present capital of Japan began as a small **settlement** where a warrior built a castle in 1457. A town named Edo grew around the castle. By the 1800s Edo had become one of the great cities of the world, with around a million inhabitants. In 1868 the Japanese emperor moved to Edo and renamed it Tokyo, which means "eastern capital."

The emperor's palace was built on the grounds of the castle. Today it is one of the few old buildings in Tokyo.

FACTS

POPULATION   25,000,000
LOCATION   eastern Honshu island, Japan, Asia
YEAR FOUNDED   1457

Busy modern life

Tokyo was badly damaged by bombs in World War II (1939-45). Now it is a modern city full of stores, offices, factories, and homes. Many of the city's separate districts have their own distinctive character.

The most popular shopping area is called the Ginza, which has large department stores, boutiques, and movie theaters. Nearby are traditional Japanese theaters. In the Akihabara district, Tokyoites and tourists buy Japanese electronic goods.

The Ginza district is 4 miles (6 km) across the city from Shibuya. The best way to get there is by using the subway.

São Paulo

São Paulo lies near the Atlantic coast of south-eastern Brazil, just south of the **Tropic of Capricorn**. With over 18 million inhabitants, it is the largest city in South America. São Paulo lies 2,400 feet (730 m) above sea level on a high **plateau** in the hills of the Serra do Mar, which means "mountains of the sea."

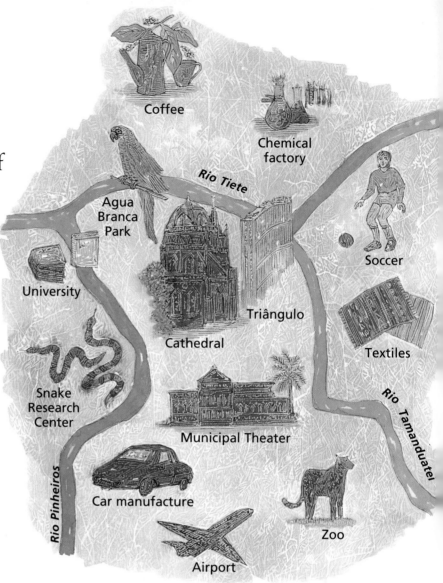

Coffee

Chemical factory

Rio Tiete

Agua Branca Park

Soccer

University

Triângulo

Cathedral

Textiles

Rio Tamanduatei

Snake Research Center

Municipal Theater

Rio Pinheiros

Car manufacture

Zoo

Airport

Central São Paulo is full of wide avenues and tall skyscrapers. If this huge city continues growing at its present rate, 25 million people will live there by the year 2010.

Portuguese settlement

In 1500 the explorer Pedro Alvares Cabral claimed Brazil for Portugal. Roman Catholic **missionaries** from Portugal founded São Paulo in 1554.

Coffee plantations began to develop in the countryside around São Paulo and the city soon became the center of Brazil's coffee industry.

The business triangle

Brazil is still the world's biggest producer of coffee. Today São Paulo also produces almost half of Brazil's industrial goods. The city's business center is called the Triângulo, "the triangle." The name comes from the original settlement, where three mission buildings were linked by paths that formed a triangle.

The people of São Paulo, who are known as Paulistas, often meet in Patriots' Square in the Triângulo. Every January 25th they celebrate the founding of their city.

Paulistas living in this shanty suburb have a view of the high-rise apartments and more luxurious buildings of the city center.

Rich and poor

Some Paulistas descended from the Indian peoples of the region, and others from Portuguese and other European **immigrants**. Many are mestizos, people of mixed Indian and European descent. São Paulo is growing fast because Brazilians come from all over to look for work.

Millions of Paulistas have no jobs or earn very little money. They live in shacks in sprawling **shanty** suburbs. Rich and poor live close together, but in separate districts.

FACTS

POPULATION	18,100,000
LOCATION	southeast Brazil, South America
YEAR FOUNDED	1554

New York

The Statue of Liberty stands on Liberty Island, in New York Bay, welcoming visitors to the largest city in the United States. It is often called New York City to distinguish it from the state of New York. It is also known by its nickname, the "Big Apple." New York City joins with other cities to form a large conurbation, with a population of more than 18 million people.

The Statue of Liberty rises 305 feet (93 m) above the water. Built in France, the statue was shipped across the Atlantic Ocean in pieces, and put together in New York in 1886.

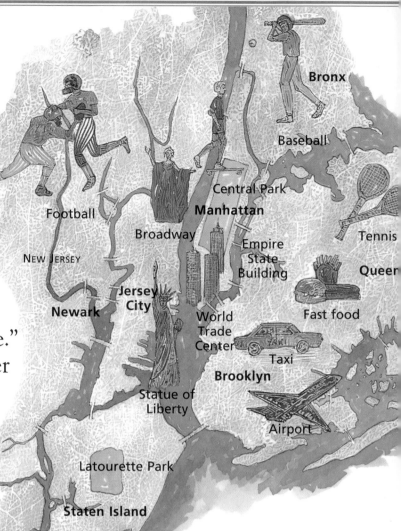

Bronx

Baseball

Central Park

Manhattan

Football

Broadway

NEW JERSEY

Empire State Building

Tennis

Queen

Jersey City

Newark

Fast food

World Trade Center

Taxi

Brooklyn

Statue of Liberty

Airport

Latourette Park

Staten Island

New Amsterdam, New York

The first people to settle here were Algonquian Indians, who lived in villages of bark huts. In 1624 Dutch **settlers** arrived, and one year later they founded New Amsterdam on the island of Manhattan. In 1626 the governor of the Dutch **colony** is said to have bought the whole island from the Indians with beads, knives, and trinkets.

In 1664 the Dutch surrendered their town to the English, who renamed it New York in honor of the Duke of York, brother of King Charles II. The city remained British until the end of the **American Revolution**, in 1783.

Around the five boroughs

Today the city of New York is made up of five sections, called boroughs. They are Manhattan, Brooklyn, Queens, Staten Island, and the Bronx. Some of the boroughs are linked by bridges, such as the Brooklyn Bridge, which links Manhattan and Brooklyn. The George Washington Bridge carries people between Manhattan and New Jersey.

Tunnels, ferries, and an underground railroad, called the subway, also connect the boroughs. The subway runs all day along 240 miles (383 km) of track, between 469 stations.

FACTS

POPULATION	18,000,000
LOCATION	southeast New York State, U.S., North America
YEAR FOUNDED	1625

The World Trade Center towers over the financial district of southern Manhattan. You can travel from here to Staten Island by ferry.

Manhattan skyline

New York's famous skyline includes many spectacular skyscrapers. They are all south of Central Park, on Manhattan island. The tallest skyscraper, the twin-towered World Trade Center, has 110 stories and rises to 1,350 feet (411 m).

The world's largest railroad station, Grand Central Terminal, and the headquarters of the United Nations are also in Manhattan. The United Nations is an international organization that promotes peace between nations.

Mexico City

Mexico City, the capital of the **Republic** of Mexico, lies 7,575 feet (2,309 m) above sea level and is the highest of the world's big cities. Mountains rise all around it, including the snow-capped peaks of two volcanoes. The mountains trap the fumes churned out by 30,000 factories and 3 million cars, and a blanket of **smog** often hangs over the city.

Aztec ruins

Textiles

Tortilla

Nezahualcoyotl

Mariachi band

Airport

Museum of Anthropology

Independence Monument

Craft market

Olympic Stadium

University

Floating Gardens

Tenochtitlán was a city of islands connected by **canals**. The waterways of Xochimilco, to the south of Mexico City, are all that is left of the Aztec canals.

Capital of the Aztecs

Modern Mexico City was built on the ruins of the capital of the Aztec **empire**. According to legend, a god told the Aztec Indians to settle where they saw a special sign – an eagle on a cactus grasping a snake.

In 1325 they found what they were looking for and built the city of Tenochtitlán. The city was destroyed by Spanish **conquerors** 200 years later. The Spanish ruled the city until 1821, when Mexico won its independence.

In this view of Mexico City on a clear day, you can look across the main square to the distant mountains. When the smog is bad, you cannot see the mountains at all.

Districts and squares

Mexico City has more than 350 districts. Many districts have their own public square, called a **plaza**, which is surrounded by many important buildings, stores, and restaurants.

Mexico City's main square is called the Zocalo. On one side is the National Palace, where the Mexican president has offices. Above the doorway hangs Mexico's Liberty Bell. Every September 15 the president rings this bell in memory of the country's bitter struggle for independence.

FACTS

POPULATION	15,100,000
LOCATION	Central Mexico, North America
YEAR FOUNDED	1325

University city

The University of Mexico lies on the southern outskirts of the city. It was founded in 1551, shortly after Mexico became a Spanish colony. It moved to its new **campus**, called University City, 400 years later. The new university buildings were designed and decorated by the country's leading artists and architects and contain some of Mexico's most beautiful **murals**.

Los Angeles

Los Angeles, the second biggest city in the U.S., sprawls over a large area near the Pacific coast of southern California. The city is called L.A. for short, but its original name was much longer. The Spanish founder of the settlement called it El Pueblo de Nuestra Señora la Reina de Los Angeles de Porciuncula – "the Town of Our Lady the Queen of the Angels of Porciuncula!"

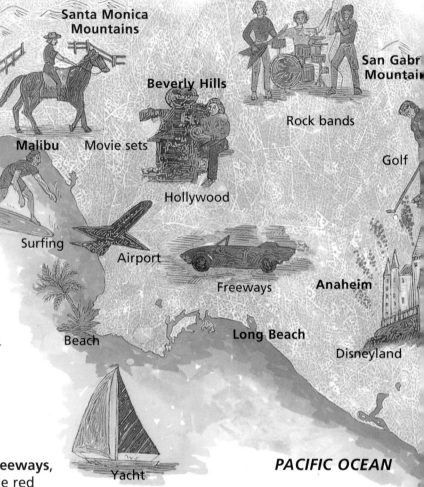

Santa Monica Mountains

Beverly Hills

San Gabr Mountai

Rock bands

Golf

Malibu

Movie sets

Hollywood

Surfing

Airport

Freeways

Anaheim

Beach

Long Beach

Disneyland

Yacht

PACIFIC OCEAN

A network of **multilane** roads, called **freeways**, links Los Angeles' different suburbs. The red lines in the photograph are made by cars' rear lights and the white lines by headlights.

Growing settlement

Los Angeles is the youngest of the world's top ten cities. The first people t live in the area were Shoshone Indians In 1771 Roman Catholic missionaries arrived from Spain, and ten years later the town was founded. It grew slowly until settlers started to pour in when the railroad arrived in 1876. Soon afterward oil was discovered, and this brought many businesses to the town.

During the last hundred years, huge numbers of tourists have been drawn to the region's warm, sunny climate.

City of suburbs

There are so many suburbs in Los Angeles that people have called it "a hundred suburbs in search of a city." Some suburbs grew up with the movie industry. Early this century **studios** were built in the suburb of Hollywood, and before long it became the movie capital of the world. Studios were also built in nearby Burbank, and Beverly Hills, another suburb, became the luxurious home of many movie stars.

Walt Disney built his first **theme park**, called Disneyland, in 1955. Disneyland is found in Anaheim, a city within the Los Angeles conurbation. This famous park is still a huge attraction today.

FACTS

POPULATION	14,500,000
LOCATION	southern California, U.S., North America
YEAR FOUNDED	1781

Environmental problems

The city suffers many environmental problems. Like Mexico City, Los Angeles has mountains on three sides and is often covered by a layer of smog. The government is trying to control car fumes and reduce **pollution** from factories. In 1993 a subway opened to help ease the city's traffic jams.

The people of Los Angeles face the constant threat of earthquakes because the city lies near the San Andreas **fault**. In 1994 a huge earthquake killed 57 people and left 25,000 homeless.

Los Angeles' freeways have lots of underpasses, overpasses, and **interchanges**. This highway collapsed during the terrible 1994 earthquake.

17

Shanghai

Shanghai is the largest city and busiest **port** in China. Its name means "on the sea," and it lies near the **mouth** of the Chang Jiang River (sometimes called the Yangtze), where it flows into the East China Sea. Along with China's capital, Beijing, it is one of the fastest growing cities in the world.

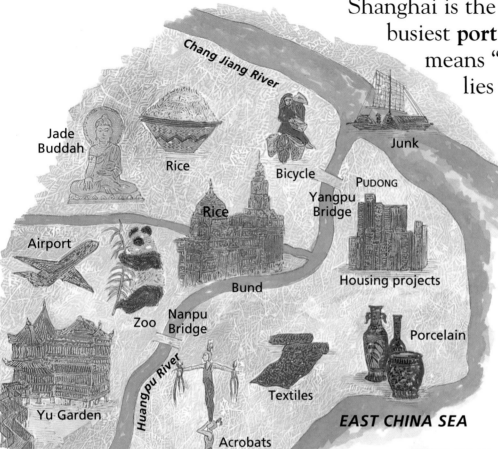

Chang Jiang River

Jade Buddah

Rice

Bicycle

Junk

PUDONG

Yangpu Bridge

Rice

Airport

Housing projects

Bund

Porcelain

Zoo

Nanpu Bridge

Huangpu River

Yu Garden

Textiles

EAST CHINA SEA

Acrobats

Trading center

Shanghai began as a small trading settlement about 800 years ago. For hundreds of years, it remained a small town on the banks of the Huangpu River, which flows into the Chang Jiang. In 1842 China was forced by Great Britain to open the town to foreign **trade**. Shanghai soon became an important trading center for many nations. Foreigners moved in to set up businesses, and Chinese **peasants** moved to the city to find work. The city grew very quickly.

Many of the streets in the old town have not changed since it was opened to foreigners. They are narrow and crowded with cyclists and pedestrians.

The Huangpu River flows through Shanghai. Here a ship passes famous buildings on the avenue formerly known as the Bund.

Chinese City

Shanghai's history can be seen today in different parts of the city. The oldest section is in the south and is often called the Chinese City. It was once surrounded by a great wall, but this was torn down in 1914. The narrow, twisting streets of the old city are very crowded.

Farther north is the old foreign section of the city, which buzzed with business for nearly a century. Along the bank of the river lies Zhong Shan Road. This impressive **avenue** has a line of grand buildings that look like those in old European cities. Many of these buildings are now used as Chinese government offices.

FACTS

POPULATION · 13,400,000
LOCATION · East China Sea coast, China, Asia
YEAR FOUNDED · about 1200

New industrial zone

The number of people living in Shanghai has doubled in the past 40 years. Completely new sections of the city have been built. On the eastern side of the Huangpu is Pudong New Area, a 135 square mile (350 sq km) zone of industrial parks, foreign factories, and high-rise apartments. More and more workers and their families are moving to this new **industrial zone** in the suburbs. Many international companies are moving into the city center.

Cairo

Cairo is the capital city of Egypt. It lies on the banks of the world's longest river, the Nile, in the northeast region of Africa. This busy capital is the oldest of the world's top ten cities. In recent years it has grown so much that it has joined with the city of Giza, the site of the famous **pyramids**.

The Citadel, which was built in the 1170s, looms over the eastern side of the city. It contains **mosques**, palaces, and museums.

Airport

Az Zamalik

Cotton

Bazaar

Cairo Tower

Mosque

Felucca

Saladin's Wal

Citade

Minarets

Cairenes

Tombs

Pyramids

Giza

Sphinx

Desert

Nile River

University

Victorious city

In A.D. 969 Fatimid Arabs from Tunisia conquered Egypt and built a new walled city as capital of their empire. They called the city Al Qáhira, "the victorious" which in English became Cairo. The city remained under Muslim rule until 1517, when it was captured by the Turks. In 1882 the British took over and ruled the city for 40 years. By the time Egypt became a republic, in 1953, Cairo's population had grown to 3 million.

On the Nile

Today the conurbation of Cairo contains more than four times as many people as it did in 1953. The population has grown so quickly that there is not enough housing for all the people. Many poor people live in makeshift shelters on rooftops, on small boats on the Nile, or in the ancient burial grounds called the City of the Dead.

Most people stay as close to the Nile as possible because it is a good source of water. Beyond the city is desert, where water and food are very scarce.

A view of Cairo from Az Zamalik, an island that divides the Nile into two channels. Six bridges connect the island to the rest of the city.

FACTS

POPULATION	13,300,000
LOCATION	northern Egypt, Africa
YEAR FOUNDED	A.D. 969

Bustling bazaars

Many of Cairo's narrow streets are crowded with markets, called bazaars. The oldest bazaar is called Khan al Khalili. It grew up around an inn built in the ancient walled city in 1382. Its maze of streets is lined with cafés and small shops selling all sorts of crafts, perfumes, and spices.

Cairo's old districts also have more than 300 mosques, where Muslims go regularly to worship.

Bombay

Bombay lies on a group of connected islands on the west coast of India. It is the nation's biggest port and major business center, and is the capital of the state of Maharashtra. The city is still growing rapidly, and new suburbs are being developed on the mainland. Bombay will probably have more than 20 million inhabitants by 2010.

Gateway to Asia

People have lived in this region since prehistoric times. A settlement was founded here in 1534, when the Sultan of Gujarat gave the islands to the Portuguese. They called the settlement Bom Bahia, or "good bay." The islands became British in 1661 and remained under British rule until India gained independence in 1947.

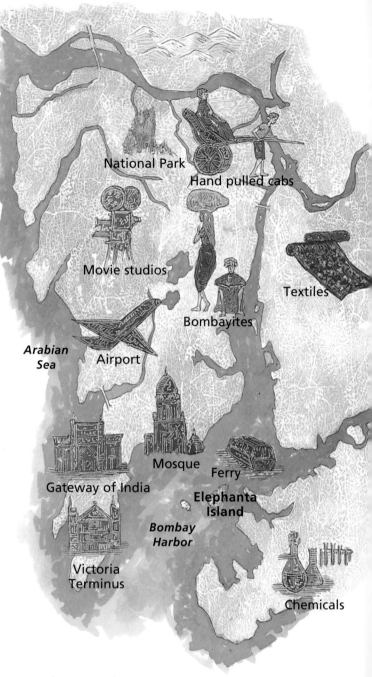

National Park

Hand pulled cabs

Movie studios

Textiles

Bombayites

Arabian Sea

Airport

Mosque

Ferry

Gateway of India

Elephanta Island

Bombay Harbor

Victoria Terminus

Chemicals

Marine Drive curves its way around Back Bay, at the southern tip of the island city. Bombay is still growing upward and outward.

Industry and business

Cotton textiles have always been an important part of Bombay's industry, but in recent years factories have opened that produce a variety of things, such as electronic goods, plastics, and chemicals. Many young people move to Bombay to look for work. The city is overcrowded, and lots of people sleep on the streets or live in shacks.

Office workers who commute on overcrowded trains have their homemade lunches delivered to them at work. Each lunch has a special marking so that it is delivered to the right person and place.

Part of the highly decorated front of Victoria Terminus railroad station which opened in 1887. It lies in a business district known as the Fort.

FACTS

POPULATION	12,600,000
LOCATION	western India, Asia
YEAR FOUNDED	1534

Hollywood of India

Bombay is the center of India's movie industry. Over 900 full-length movies are produced in India every year, and many of them are made in Bombay. They are mostly action-packed adventures, full of traditional singing and dancing.

The people of Bombay love going to the movies, and streets display brightly-painted posters advertising the latest Bombay blockbusters.

Buenos Aires

Buenos Aires is the capital and largest city of Argentina. It lies on the **estuary** of the river called Rio de la Plata, where the Paraná and Uruguay rivers flow into the Atlantic Ocean. Buenos Aires is Argentina's major port and home to more than one-third of the nation's people.

Port

Rugby

Colón Theater

Rio de la Plata

Obelisk

Opera

Tango dancers

La Boca

Textiles

Ballet

Soccer

Rio Riachuelo

Airport

Spanish colony

Spanish sailors founded the settlement in 1536. They named it after their patron saint of fair winds, Nuestra Señora Santa Maria del Buen Aire, "Our Lady Saint Mary of the Fair Wind." In 1776 the town became the capital of several Spanish colonies in South America. Forty years later the region declared its independence. The population was about 100,000 by 1850, and 50 years later it had grown to almost a million.

The Avenida 9 de Julio (Avenue of July 9th) runs through the city. At 430 feet (130 m), it is one of the widest streets in the world.

People of the port

The inhabitants of Buenos Aires are known as porteños, "people of the port." Most are of Spanish descent. At the end of the nineteenth century and the beginning of this century, the porteños built wide avenues and beautiful, spacious buildings in their city. These are still seen today.

As the city spread out, new **residential districts**, called barrios, grew up. Today there are about 50 separate districts, each with its own history and character.

There are many wealthy sections as well as slum areas where poor people live. One of the best-known workers' districts is called La Boca. It is famous for its brightly-painted sheet-iron houses and its soccer team, Boca Juniors.

Some of the colorful houses of La Boca, in the eastern part of the city near the waterfront. Many immigrants have settled here, and the district is well known for its Italian restaurants

FACTS

POPULATION	12,500,000
LOCATION	northeast Argentina, South America
YEAR FOUNDED	1536

Music and dance

Buenos Aires is Argentina's cultural center. It is a city of music, theater, museums, and libraries. International opera stars come to the beautiful Colón Theater to sing. Argentina's national symphony orchestra and ballet company perform in this opera house. Buenos Aires is also the home of the tango, a gliding Latin American dance that first became popular in the 1880s.

Rio de Janeiro

Rio de Janeiro, which is often simply called Rio, is the second largest city in Brazil and the tenth largest in the world. It lies on the Atlantic coast, 240 miles (380 km) north of São Paulo. Rio has one of the most beautiful settings of any of the world's cities. It lies between green, forested mountains and the blue ocean, and is fringed by golden, sandy beaches.

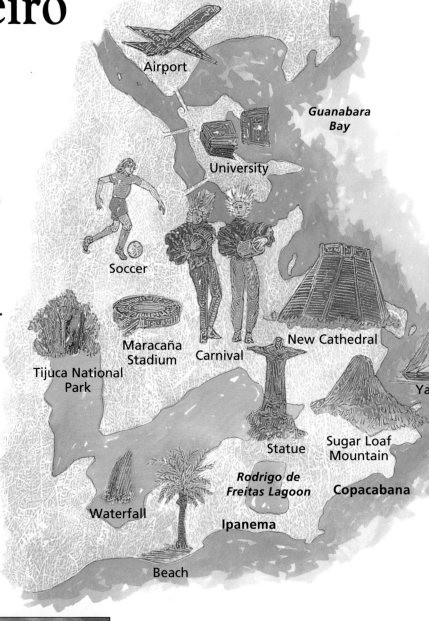

Airport

Guanabara Bay

University

Soccer

Maracaña Stadium

Carnival

New Cathedral

Tijuca National Park

Statue

Sugar Loaf Mountain

Ya

Waterfall

Rodrigo de Freitas Lagoon

Copacabana

Ipanema

Beach

A view from Sugar Loaf Mountain, across the bay to the 2,300 foot (700 m) high peak of Corcovado. A statue of Christ looks down on the city.

River of January

When Portuguese explorers first arrived in 1503, they thought Guanabara Bay was the mouth of a big river. They named the area after the month in which they found it: Rio de Janeiro means "River of January." When Brazil became independent in 1822, Rio was made its capital. In 1960 a new capital, Brasilia, was built closer to the center of the country.

On the hillside

The people of Rio are known as Cariocas, a word that comes from the language of the Tupi Indians, Rio's original inhabitants. Rich Cariocas live in luxury around Rio's beaches and **lagoons**, such as Copacabana. But almost a million poor Cariocas live in makeshift shacks on the steep hillsides. These shanty settlements are called favelas, after a wild flower that grows on the hills.

Here squatters live in shacks made of wood, corrugated iron, or cardboard. There is no running water or **sewerage**, and rain can often bring dangerous mudslides and floods. Rio is a city of great contrasts between rich and poor.

Poor houses and flimsy shacks cover many of the hills overlooking the beautiful Rio beaches of Copacabana and Ipanema.

FACTS

POPULATION	11,100,000
LOCATION	southeast Brazil, South America
YEAR FOUNDED	1565

Carnival time

Cariocas pride themselves on knowing how to have fun. Every year, just before the Christian season of Lent, they celebrate Carnival, a festival of four days and nights of amazing parades, colorful costumes, and dancing in the streets. Another favorite pastime is watching soccer at Rio's vast Maracaña stadium that once held over 199,000 spectators for a World Cup match. Locals and tourists also spend much of their time on the beach.

The World's Cities

The ten biggest cities are spread around the world's **continents**. Three of the cities are in Asia, the biggest continent. Three are in North America, and three more in South America. Just one, Cairo, lies on the continent of Africa. But there are big, important cities in Europe and Australia, too.

Sydney

Sydney is the oldest and biggest city in Australia. It was founded as a city when the first European settlers arrived in 1788, although **Aborigines** had been living in the region for thousands of years.

Today one of Australia's most famous sights is the Sydney Opera House (right), which opened in 1973. The roofs of the building were designed to look like giant sails.

Paris

Today Europe's largest city is Paris, the capital of France, with a population of just over 9 million. Paris was founded in Roman times, on a small island in the middle of the Seine River. By 1900 it was the third largest city in the world, after London and New York.

One of the most famous Parisian landmarks is the Eiffel Tower (left). This 984 foot (300 m) tower was the tallest building in the world when it was completed in 1889.

London

When the Romans came to Great Britain in A.D. 43, they built a town on the banks of the Thames River and called it Londinium. Eventually it grew into London, today's capital of the United Kingdom.

Now London has almost 8 million inhabitants. The clock tower and bell of London's Houses of Parliament (above) are known as "Big Ben." This famous clock started keeping time in 1859.

Johannesburg

Johannesburg was founded in 1886 when gold was found in the area. The city grew fast and soon became the center of South Africa's goldmining industry. Today it is the largest city in the Republic of South Africa and about 4 million people live there. In 1994 Johannesburg was made capital of the new province of Gauteng.

Glossary

The Emperor's Palace in Tokyo.

Aborigines The original inhabitants of Australia

American Revolution The war from 1775 to 1783, in which the Americans defeated the British to become independent and form the United States

avenue A wide road lined with trees

campus The grounds and buildings of a university

canal A constructed waterway

colony The community formed by a group of people who go to live in a new country

conqueror A soldier who goes to a foreign country to gain contol of it

continent One of the Earth's huge land masses

conurbation A large built-up sprawl, where towns and cities grow until they are joined together

empire The territory ruled over by an emperor

Equator An imaginary circle around the middle of the Earth

estuary The wide part of a river at its mouth, where the river's freshwater mixes with the sea's saltwater

fault A fracture in the Earth's surface, where earthquakes often occur

freeway A large road with many lanes; a highway

immigrant A person who comes from a foreign country to live permanently

industrial zone An area of factories and businesses

The city of Los Angeles lies near the San Andreas fault.

inhabitant A person who lives in a particular place

interchange A junction of roads

lagoon A pool of water cut off from the sea

missionary Someone who teaches people in another country or region about religion

A beautiful mural from Mexico City.

mosque A place of worship for Muslims, followers of the Islamic religion

mouth The end of a river, where it flows into the sea

multilane A road with many lanes

mural A wall painting

peasant A person who works on the land

plateau A flat area of land

plaza A public square

pollution Damage caused by poisonous and harmful substances

port A city with a large harbor on a body of water

pyramid A huge stone construction with sides that slope to a point

republic A country with a president elected by the people

residential district An area of a city where people have their homes

settlement A place where people settle and live together

settler A person who goes to live in a new country

sewerage Drains that take away water and waste matter

shanty A poorly built hut that serves as a home

skyscraper A very tall building

smog (From **sm**oke and **fog**.) A mixture of smoke, fog, and fumes

studio A large building in which movies are made

suburb A district at the edge of a city

theme park An area of entertainments and attractions, where the activities are based on a theme

trade Business; buying and selling goods

Tropic of Capricorn An imaginary line that stretches around the Earth, south of the Equator

Women trade at a market stall in Cairo.

Index

All words in **bold** appear in the glossary on pages 30-31